FAVOURITE MOTOR CAR STORIES

Barbara Hayes
Illustrated by J.B. Long

TREASURE PRESS

D0256751

First published in Great Britain in 1986 by Octopus Books Ltd
as four separate volumes under the titles *Freddy the Ford,*
Micky the MG, Bertie the Bentley and *Maurice Minor*

This omnibus edition published in 1991 by
Treasure Press
Michelin House
81 Fulham Road
London SW3 6RB

ISBN   1 85051 641 3

Printed in Hong Kong

FREDDY THE FORD

This is the story
of how Freddy the Ford left his
hard-working life at the car hire lot
in Hollywood and travelled across
the Atlantic Ocean to find a happier
home in England with the famous
rich adventurer Sir Robert
Rutherford.

Freddy the little green Ford opened his eyes and blinked at the sun shining down from a clear blue sky. 'Well, pals,' he said to the other cars, 'here comes another day. Let's look cheerful about it.'

The other cars tried to smile. 'Perhaps we shall be hired by nice kind people today,' they said, 'if we are lucky.'

They all lived on Pete's Car Hire lot in Hollywood. Almost every day they were hired out to different people. It was not an easy life.

People did not mean to be unkind. They were just thoughtless. One day a jolly young fellow hired Freddy the Ford. At first Freddy was pleased. The young man was a good driver. 'This will be a pleasant day out,' thought Freddy.

How wrong he was! The young fellow packed the car with friends, then roared non-stop up and down the hilly roads outside the city.

'Fun runs', they called the rides, but they were not much fun for puffing, groaning Freddy.

But cheery little Freddy kept on smiling. 'I always try to look on the bright side,' he would say.

However even Freddy grew impatient with one dreamy young couple. They hired him for a whole month's holiday and would say things like: 'Let's go up that road, it looks so pretty.'

Then, without bothering about little things such as checking the fuel tank, they would set off along a hot desert road. Time after time Freddy was left gasping while the young couple had to walk for petrol.

'Oh well, it takes all sorts to make a world!' smiled brave, little Freddy. 'I hope my next customers take me somewhere cool.'

His wish was granted, only too well! A family hired Freddy to drive them to their log cabin high up in the mountains. 'We don't want to ruin our own car on these steep, icy roads,' they said, 'but it doesn't matter what happens to a hire car.'

'Thank you very much!' thought Freddy, as he shivered all night in the snow outside the cosy cabin.

Pete Hacker, the owner of the car hire firm, often used to say: 'That Ford is a great goer. Always cheerful and willing. It seems a shame he's forever going out with people who don't appreciate him, but that's life I guess!'

Then one day everything changed. A tall, bold-looking man with red hair strode into the car lot and put his hand on Freddy's bonnet. His name was Sir Robert Rutherford. 'I should like to hire this cheery little Ford,' he said to Pete.

A deal was struck. Sir Robert sat at the wheel and Freddy the Ford's life of happiness began.

Sir Robert was a rich adventurer, who liked to roam the world looking for thrills. Just now he was enjoying being a Hollywood film actor, playing in all sorts of exciting stories.

He drove Freddy in through the gates of The Legend Film Company and the little Ford smiled graciously as the gate keeper saluted them. 'Fordy,' said Sir Robert, 'you and I are going to have fun!'

Never a truer word was spoken! Everywhere that Sir Robert went, Freddy – or 'Fordy' as Sir Robert called him – went too. Once Freddy felt quite scared when he saw Sir Robert dressed up like an ancient Roman and fighting a real lion.

'Don't worry, young Fordy,' said the director of the film, as he stood at Freddy's side. 'It's all acting, just pretending you know. That lion is too old to hurt a fly. He's not thinking about anything but the meal he will get when the scene is over.'

9

All the same Freddy was much happier when the next film came along. It was all about pirates attacking an old fort. Freddy stood on the quayside watching the guns on the ship blaze and listening to the cannon of the fort reply: 'BOOM! BOOM!'

Water splashed. Smoke rose into the air. The camera crew stood on a little jetty and filmed all the action.

Freddy had never felt more contented. He was well cared for, with plenty of petrol in his tank and cool water in his radiator. How long could it all last?

Sometimes Freddy woke in the night and wondered what would happen when Sir Robert left Hollywood. Would he be sent back to the car hire lot? Freddy the Ford shuddered and pushed the idea to the back of his mind.

'I must enjoy each day as it comes. Always look on the bright side, that's what I say,' he thought.

That day Sir Robert played the part of a cavalryman whose horse bolted with some wild ones and had to be recaptured with a lassoo. It looked very dangerous!

Freddy did not spend all his time at the film studios. When they were not working, he and Sir Robert lazed in a beautiful Hollywood home with green lawns and a swimming pool.

There were always lots of parties and fun and laughter in the sunshine. But no matter how many guests he had, Sir Robert always found a moment to speak to Freddy. 'Having a nice rest, Fordy old chap?' he would ask. 'Back to work on Monday, you know.' Freddy would smile with happiness.

But Sir Robert was a restless man. One morning he woke up and thought: 'I've done enough filming. I'm bored with Hollywood. I want to go to New York!'

He finished his film, paid another month's rent on the beautiful house and drove Freddy back to Pete's Hire Car lot.

'I know Fordy isn't the grandest car in the world,' Sir Robert said to Pete, 'but I like his cheery face. Will you sell him to me?' Freddy almost jumped with joy when Pete said 'Yes.'

Sir Robert drove Freddy to the best garage in town and spoke to the chief mechanic. 'I want Fordy completely overhauled,' he said. 'Everything is to be put right and everything is to be serviced properly, with no expense spared.'

Sir Robert was like that. He was not much of a mechanic himself, but he knew that cars had to be treated right. He was a good owner.

'Yes, sir,' replied the mechanic with a cheery salute, and opening his bag of tools, he set to work.

Freddy the Ford felt wonderful after his overhaul. He was driven back to Sir Robert Rutherford's rented house and stood in the garden wondering whatever would happen next.

'EEEEK!' he squealed as a shower of cold water suddenly splashed all over him.

'My orders are to keep you washed down every day and have you smart and clean, ready to leave at a moment's notice,' explained Harold the handyman.

Up in the house, Sir Robert was busy on the phone.

For several days Freddy stood in the garden taking life easy – except for his daily cold shower!

Then at last, Sir Robert came out of the house smiling. 'Everything is fixed, Fordy my lad,' he said. 'I am going to act in a theatre on Broadway, in New York, and you and I will drive all the way across America to get there!'

What an adventure! The two pals drove over the mountains and across the great plains. Sometimes it seemed like too great a journey for such a little car.

But no matter how long the road, nor how steep the hill, Freddy kept going. Nothing would allow him to let down his kind new owner.

Every evening as they drove, hobbled or limped into some small town, Sir Robert would hail a passerby and ask: 'Can you direct me to the best garage please? This great little Ford is driving me all across America and only the best is good enough for him.' Only when Freddy was taken care of would Sir Robert look for a hotel for himself.

At last the great journey was over and Freddy and Sir Robert arrived safely in New York. Sir Robert rented another fine house and was a big success when the play opened on Broadway. Photographers and reporters flocked round to the house.

'Why don't you get yourself a swankier car than this little tin can?' asked one of the reporters.

'Fordy and I are pals,' explained Sir Robert firmly, 'and I'll thank you not to refer to any friend of mine as a tin can.'

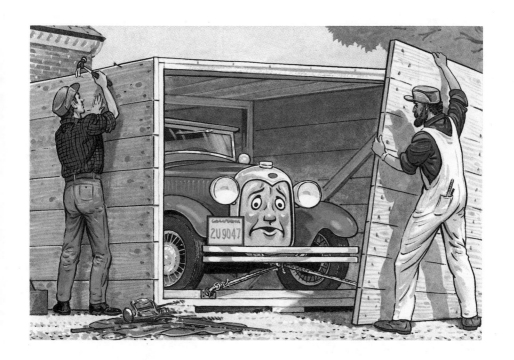

Life ran along smoothly for several months. Then one day, Sir Robert announced to Freddy: 'Fordy, old chap, the play is finishing. We're going home. Be prepared for a long journey.'

'Oh goody!' thought Freddy, imagining another great drive all the way back across America.

But instead of setting out on the open road, Freddy found his engine being drained. Next thing he was being nailed up into a wooden crate – BANG! BANG! BANG! How his poor head ached!

Freddy felt bewildered. Where was he going? Where *was* Sir Robert's home? Then he overheard one of the workmen: 'Fancy bothering to take this car all the way to England. That guy must be fond of it, that's all I can say!'

England! Freddie tried to remember where England was. A little island far, far across the sea, was all he knew. So Sir Robert's home was in England!

Then the crate was lifted on to a truck and driven to the dockside where it was loaded into a big cargo boat.

'Oh my goodness! What will become of me?' gasped Freddy. 'All alone on a great big boat! Suppose it loses its way! Or sinks!'

Then Freddy calmed down: 'Silly me! Everything must be all right. Sir Robert would never send me anywhere unsafe. This must be a fine, strong boat and the captain is *sure* to know the way to England. I expect Sir Robert had a special word with him and told him to be *certain* not to sink while *I* am on board!'

Soon the ship was out on the open ocean.

Crossing the Atlantic Ocean took several days. The seas were rough. The cargo boat rolled from the crest of one wave down into the trough of another, then up to the next crest and down again to the next trough.

Up – down! Up – down! Up – down!

Tucked away in the hold in his wooden crate, Freddy did not feel well, but he would not admit that he felt sick. He liked to keep cheerful.

'Groan! Gulp! I feel fine,' he moaned. 'Oooh! Ugh! Life's great!'

At last the boat stopped rolling and chugged into the calm waters of a harbour. 'Whew! Thank goodness!' gasped Freddy.

He felt his crate being unloaded and taken on a journey. Then – BUMP! – it was dumped on to the ground. There was a lot of squeaking and creaking and puffing and panting as workmen pulled the nails from the crate and took down the sides. Freddy blinked in the sudden bright daylight. He looked round at his new home, and liked what he saw.

'It seems I'm still in luck!' grinned Freddy. And he was. Sir Robert's home was surrounded with large gardens and had stables and paddocks too. Best of all there was a comfortable, dry, warm garage which Freddy was to share with a big red Rolls-Royce.

They soon became great friends, and once Freddy had been issued with a new number plate and had learnt to drive on the opposite side of the road, he and the Rolls-Royce would go to show-jumping meetings to watch Sir Robert competing.

But Sir Robert continued to be very restless. One day, Freddy noticed him taking tea on the terrace with a friend called Howard. They were studying maps, and spread around them were all the things they would need for a dangerous trip to a hot country – a rifle, sun hats, strong boots, water bottles, binoculars and a chest of hot weather clothes.

'Hmm!' thought Freddy. 'It looks as if we are about to set off on another trip.'

Little did he guess he was to be left behind!

A few weeks later Freddy drove down to the dockside with Sir Robert, Kate, his girlfriend, and Howard, but instead of being taken aboard, Freddy was left on shore with Kate as the two men boarded the big ship.

Freddy tried to keep smiling, but it was a hard job as he looked at the cranes and the tug and the seagulls, and the big ship getting smaller and smaller.

'This isn't a trip for cars.' Sir Robert had said. 'You'll see. You must wait at home!'

Kate drove Freddy home, with strict instructions from Sir Robert to keep an eye on him.

'I can't say I'm not well cared for,' sighed Freddy, but all the same he spent many wistful hours standing on the driveway looking towards the gates and the lodge house. He longed for the day when the lodge keeper would rush out to fling the gates wide apart and welcome Sir Robert home.

Everyone started to call Freddy 'Faithful Fordy' because he waited so patiently for his master.

'Hey there, Faithful Fordy,' Kate called out excitedly one morning. 'I've had a letter from Robert, all the way from South America. He and Howard have hired guides and two little canoes and are paddling up the dangerous River Amazon. General Tomsett, an explorer, was lost there five years ago and they are looking for him.'

Hearing this news Freddy felt happier at being left behind. Although only a small car, he was still too big to ride on a fragile canoe!

Many weeks passed and no more letters arrived. Everyone became very worried. Was Sir Robert lost too? Finally Kate came rushing to tell 'Faithful Fordy' that news had come at last.

'Robert has had a terrible time,' she gasped, 'but he is safe. Things started going wrong when the canoes were attacked by crocodiles. Robert fired his rifle at them to try to drive them away, but there were too many. They overturned the canoes and spilled everyone and everything into the water.'

Freddy shuddered with worry, but Kate went on:

'Luckily the men managed to cling to the upturned canoes and they were quickly swept away by the strong currents in the river. They drifted for hours until they were washed ashore by a tiny settlement far upstream. Imagine their amazement when they were greeted in English by General Tomsett! He too had just had a lucky escape and had managed to get away from the fierce jungle tribes who had held him prisoner for so long.'

The river people were friendly and helpful, and guided Sir Robert, Howard and the General back to the mouth of the River Amazon.

'Well, Freddy,' smiled Sir Robert when he eventually reached home. 'I think my adventuring days are over. It's time I settled down. What would you say if I married Kate?'

'Good idea!' tootled Freddy.

The wedding took place and as the years went by a son and a daughter joined the family.

Sir Robert became a businessman and used the red Rolls-Royce every day. Freddy became the local runabout for Kate and the children. One day when Kate was chatting to the lodge keeper, young Edward noticed Freddy looking longingly up the open road.

He patted Freddy's bonnet. 'Don't worry,' he said. 'As soon as I am old enough, you can come adventuring with me. You can be *my* Faithful Fordy!'

Freddy the Ford smiled. 'Now that is *really* something to look forward to,' he thought.

MICKY THE MG

Micky the MG
was a jolly, little red sports car. This
is the story of how he left his old
owner, Mister Greyhair, and found
new friends in Freddy the Ford and
Bertie the Bentley at beautiful
Whiteporch Manor. He found
a little trouble there, too.

Micky the MG was a little red open-topped sports car with big headlamps, a useful little fog lamp and a hooter above his number plate, and his initials – MG – on a badge below his radiator cap.

To look at him you would think he did not have a care in the world. But actually, he was looking for a new home. His owner, Mister Greyhair, who had loved and cared for him for years, was now too old to drive.

'I will run you over to Whiteporch Manor,' said Mister Greyhair. 'Jimmy Taylor might take you in.'

Years before, Jimmy Taylor had run his own garage. Now he lived in a flat at the back of Whiteporch and collected old cars as a hobby. Everybody called him Uncle Jimmy.

Micky the MG felt hopeful as they drove up the long driveway to Whiteporch Manor. 'I could be happy here,' he thought. 'I do hope that Mister Taylor will want me, but they say he is very fussy.'

As they neared the house, Micky noticed a bright new Mercedes and a Rolls-Royce in the front garage.

'They belong to Sir Alec Smoothdeal, "Smart Alec", who lives in the Manor,' said Mister Greyhair. 'He doesn't like old cars, only big modern ones.'

How the Mercedes and Rolls-Royce sneered at little Micky as he drove past!

'Goodness! I didn't know titchy old things like that were still allowed on the road,' they jeered. 'One steep hill and he'd cough to a standstill, but old Uncle Jimmy will think he's wonderful no doubt and we shall be plagued with the little brat!'

Micky pretended not to hear the spiteful chatter of the modern cars and drove round to the stable block at the back of the big house.

A friendly young man with fair hair was tinkering with the engine of a huge car even older than Micky. It was a Bentley, Bertie the Bentley he was called, as Micky later learned.

Micky looked at the well-swept yard and the businesslike tool box. 'I like everything about this place, except those cars at the front,' he thought.

The young man turned and spoke. 'Oh Mister Greyhair,' he smiled, wiping his hands, 'have you brought Micky to see if Uncle Jimmy will take him into the collection?'

'That's right,' replied Mister Greyhair. 'Micky is a good car and deserves a kind owner. I should hate to send him to a car auction where anyone might buy him.' At those words Micky became really worried. So that was what lay in store! If Uncle Jimmy did not like him, he was to be sent for sale at an auction!

Suddenly Micky heard footsteps and saw a tall man in overalls walking round the side of the stables.

'This must be Mister Taylor, "Uncle Jimmy",' thought Micky. 'My whole future depends on him. If Uncle Jimmy likes me and thinks I am fit enough, I can stay here in this nice place and make friends with that sensible-looking old Bentley. But if he finds something wrong with me, then its off to the car auction to be sold to anyone!'

He shuddered! 'I might even be sold for spares!'

Jimmy Taylor shook hands with Mister Greyhair.
'So this is the MG,' he said, nodding at Micky. 'He
looks in good condition, but of course I must give his
works a thorough check. If I like him, I will make you a
fair offer.'

'I've had him since new and taken good care of him,'
said Mister Greyhair. 'He's a great little car and never
lets you down if he's treated right.'

Micky and Bertie and the fair haired young man all
watched expectantly. Would Micky be accepted?

Mister Greyhair walked away to sit and wait while Micky was examined. Micky knew by the way Uncle Jimmy opened the bonnet and ran his hands over the engine that he had a way with cars. Even at that important moment, Micky couldn't help giggling.

'Tee-hee!' he quivered as Uncle Jimmy touched his spark plugs.

'Ticklish, I see,' grinned Uncle Jimmy, giving Micky a friendly pat. Then he became more serious as he made the rest of his thorough checks.

'That's over!' smiled Uncle Jimmy, shutting Micky's bonnet and walking over to talk to Mister Greyhair.

The young man, who was known as Tinker, took some coffee to the two men and then listened quietly. He was learning as much as possible about cars so that he could take over from Uncle Jimmy in the course of time. Micky strained to hear what was being said, but he could not.

'*Surely* I'm good enough!' he thought. 'I *feel* fit and I haven't a spot of rust anywhere.'

Micky's thoughts were interrupted by the friendly voice of the old Bentley, standing alongside.

'Don't look so worried,' smiled the big car. 'I think you have a good chance of being taken in. We cars live in the old stable block, you know, and there's a small empty space just your size near a window. It's next to where a nice American Ford car stands. I think Uncle Jimmy might well let you live there.'

'Oh, thank you. I do hope so,' said Micky, feeling happier.

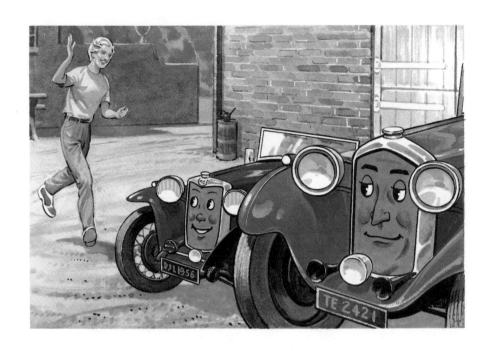

The grand old Bentley with its huge headlamps, its low-slung fog light and its fine trumpet-shaped horns, said nothing more and Micky would not dare speak until spoken to. They waited in silence until they heard a happy shout.

Tinker came running across the yard, waving and smiling. 'Good news, Micky,' he called. 'Uncle Jimmy has decided to accept you. You can stay!'

WUMP! WUMPITY!

Micky the MG's heart jumped for joy!

Tinker patted Micky the MG, and Bertie said: 'Congratulations!' in his splendid deep voice.

'I'm so pleased,' smiled Mister Greyhair to Micky. 'You have been such a faithful pal through all the years! It is wonderful to think you are going to be looked after so well in this happy place. Oh dear! Now I suppose I must be off!'

He turned and walked away, but could not hold back his tears at parting from his dear old friend.

Micky felt a lump come to his throat!

So Micky started life in his pleasant new home with Tinker and Uncle Jimmy and the other old cars. Things should have been so happy, yet they were turning out so sadly.

Micky stood alone and moped. He did not chat with the other cars. He did not have the heart to join in with their laughter.

He was sluggish when Tinker or Uncle Jimmy tried to start him up. Uncle Jimmy began to wonder if, for the first time, he had been wrong about a car.

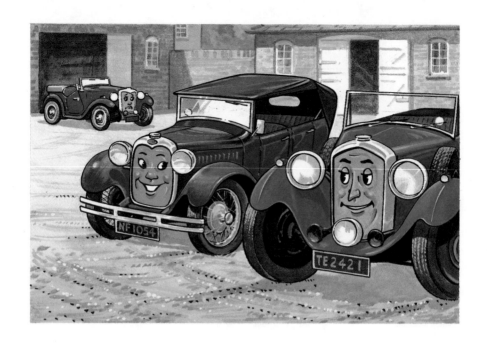

The grand old car, Bertie the Bentley, spoke to the little American car, Freddy the Ford. 'Fordy, old chap,' said Bertie, 'I'm beginning to think we've got a wrong 'un in that MG. He seemed such a brave little fellow when he arrived. I quite took to him. Now he only feels sorry for himself. If being here hasn't lived up to his expectations, he should grin and bear it, that's what I say.'

'I'll have a word with Tinker about him,' replied Freddy the Ford. 'Perhaps Micky is home-sick.'

Freddy the Ford had a kind heart. In his early life he had seen a lot of hardship and now he liked to help others in trouble.

'Tinker,' he said, the next day, when he was being polished, 'that MG seemed very fond of his old master, Mister Greyhair. Do you think he is missing him?'

'I'll try to find out,' replied Tinker. 'Something has to be done. Micky can't go on moping like this. Uncle Jimmy calls it sulking and he won't put up with much more of it.'

'It isn't so much that I miss Mister Greyhair,' explained Micky, when Tinker spoke to him. 'I'm worried that *he* is missing *me*. I have you and the others to talk to, but now he is all alone. I feel so sad for him.'

Tinker believed in going straight to the heart of a problem.

'Let's visit Mister Greyhair and find out,' he said, 'but before we go, I will take a photograph of you.'

He fetched his camera. 'Smile, please,' he said to Micky. 'SNAP!'

The photograph turned out very well and Tinker had a print framed and took it with them when he and Micky drove to visit Mister Greyhair.

'What a lovely surprise,' said Mister Greyhair, coming out through the white wooden gateway. 'I hope you are enjoying your new home, Micky.'

'I'm afraid he isn't,' replied Tinker. 'He is worried that you are missing him.'

'But I am fine,' replied Mister Greyhair. 'Now that I have no worries about Micky, I am quite content.'

'Of course I could not help shedding a tear when I parted from Micky,' smiled Mister Greyhair, 'but if he came back, I should be worried about his future again.'

He spoke sternly to Micky. 'Now look here, Micky,' he said. 'You are to behave in your new home and no more nonsense. Go back to Whiteporch and be cheerful, or you'll make everyone else unhappy.'

Tinker put the photograph of Micky on Mister Greyhair's mantelpiece as a happy reminder of the old days.

Tinker and Micky sped happily over the few miles back to Whiteporch. Now that Micky knew his old owner was happy, he could start enjoying life in his new home.

'Uncle Jimmy has collected together a really nice group of cars,' said Tinker, as they drove up the long driveway. 'Bertie is very steady and reliable. He will give you good advice; and Freddy is a cheerful chap. He always likes to look on the bright side. You should have some good laughs with him.'

Micky felt really happy again as he and Tinker drove round the front of Whiteporch, where the big new cars lived with Sir Alec Smoothdeal. Apart from being sneered at when he first arrived, Micky had had nothing to do with the modern cars. He had spent his time at the back of the house with Uncle Jimmy.

WHEEE! Tinker made a fast turn round the new Rolls parked by the front porch. Too late they saw the muddy puddle. SLOSH! It splashed all over the Rolls. He was not at all pleased!

'Sorry old chap!' called Tinker. 'I'll come back and give you a clean after I've parked Micky.'

He drove on round to the old stable block, but before he could return, Sir Alec Smoothdeal had come out of the house. Sir Alec owned the house and the estate. He ran them very well, but he was a hard, sharp man. He was furious when he saw his expensive Rolls-Royce, splattered with mud.

'That's all I need,' he shouted. 'A muddy car to drive in to meet my important business friends!'

'That little brat of an MG did it,' hissed the Rolls sneakily. At once Sir Alec rushed round the house and started shouting at Tinker.

'I'm sick of these crumbling old wrecks crawling all round the place,' he roared, pointing at Micky. 'If they can't be made to behave, they can all go to the car auction. Then I shall be rid of them for good.'

Luckily, Uncle Jimmy, who was Smart Alec's real uncle and had played with him when he was a little boy, came out and calmed everything down.

Uncle Jimmy, Sir Alec Smoothdeal, Tinker and Micky all stood in a group in the yard at the back of Whiteporch, talking.

In spite of his hard, business ways, Sir Alec was fond of his uncle. 'I'll overlook this naughtiness for your sake, Uncle Jimmy,' he said, 'but Tinker must not let it happen again. This saucy MG must be kept in order.'

The Rolls-Royce peeped round the corner, grinning slyly because he had succeeded in getting Micky into trouble.

Sir Alec Smoothdeal strode off. Uncle Jimmy turned and gave Micky a reproving tap. 'You and Tinker must be more careful,' he said. 'Richard the Rolls is spiteful and jealous. If you have made an enemy of him, he will never stop trying to get you into trouble.'

Micky was surprised. 'Richard?' he chortled.

Tinker said: 'The new Rolls is called Richard because he comes from a very grand and aristocratic family. He never allows anyone to shorten his name to Ricky.'

Luckily, Micky did not see much of Richard the Rolls for several weeks. Instead he made friends with Freddy the Ford, who stood next to him at night in their old stable garage.

Some nights when they could not sleep for the bright moonlight shining in through the window, they would stand cosily in their blankets, warmed by the electric fire on the wall above. Freddy would tell Micky stories about his early life in America, and his adventures there.

However, life at Whiteporch was not all idling and chatting. Micky had to keep fit and often went for drives round the estate with Tinker.

One day, Tinker said: 'Micky, you are strong enough to work. Today you will go to a fête and earn some money for charity.' He explained that Uncle Jimmy often sent his best cars to go on display and help raise money for good causes.

Micky felt very proud as he drove round to the front of Whiteporch Manor.

But on that bright, sunny day, luck was not with
Micky. Richard, the spiteful new Rolls-Royce, had
seen him coming and was waiting for him.

Richard puffed and panted until he managed to push
off his handbrake. Then, just as Tinker drove Micky
round in front of him, Richard lurched forward.

He was much bigger and heavier than little Micky,
and he meant to crush him. Tinker, not expecting the
Rolls to move, noticed nothing, but Micky did.

He gasped with dismay.

Poor little Micky thought that his last moment had come. Suddenly a haughty voice boomed across the drive: 'That's quite enough of that, young Richard. Back up and behave yourself!'

It was the Duchess, the oldest Rolls-Royce in Uncle Jimmy's collection, who had appeared as if from nowhere. She had a tall old-fashioned radiator with a real silver lady gracefully perched on top. All her chrome gleamed and shone. Her bronze-coloured coachwork was polished like new.

Uncle Jimmy was driving the Duchess, who had also been chosen to go to the charity fête with Micky.

Richard the Rolls slunk back into his place. 'Sorry, Duchess,' he mumbled.

'Bullying little cars is not the way a gentleman should behave,' purred the Duchess, as Uncle Jimmy drove her past Richard. 'Sometimes I wonder if you really *are* a Rolls at all.'

Micky hurried on his way, thankful that the magnificent old Duchess had come to his aid.

The Duchess and Micky stood side by side at the charity fête.

'Thank you for protecting me from Richard,' Micky dared to whisper to the grand, proud, old car.

'You are a bright, brave little fellow,' replied the Duchess. 'You should do well in the collection as long as you do not get too cheeky. I will keep a friendly eye on you and I am sure you will be happy.'

'Oh, I shall be, I *shall*,' smiled Micky.

And he *was*.

BERTIE THE BENTLEY

Bertie the Bentley was as happy as a car could be. He had a kind owner who took him on lots of interesting jaunts. Then when war came life changed suddenly — for the worst! This is the story of how Bertie narrowly misses the scrap yard and goes on to save a man's life!

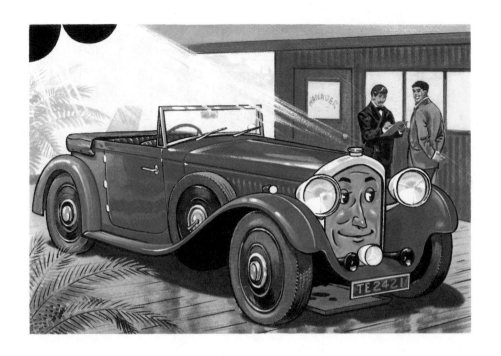

Bertie the Bentley was brand new, and very powerful. His great headlamps glared from either side of his face. His foglight stood at the ready between two black horns. Bertie was big and tough, but he was patient and even-tempered too. He was a fine car.

Jimmy Taylor was looking for a new car. He walked into the London Car Show Rooms where Bertie stood, shiny and eager to go.

'That is the car for me,' said Mister Taylor to the salesman. 'I like his style.'

So started the long friendship between Jimmy Taylor, who was a clever engineer, and Bertie the Bentley.

'You're coming to a good home, Bentley my lad,' smiled Jimmy, as he drove Bertie through the green English countryside to a pretty, stone house on a busy country road.

Bertie was pleased to see a garage next to his new home. 'That's handy for servicing,' he thought, not realizing the garage belonged to his new owner.

Life was wonderful for Bertie the Bentley in those early years. Living next door to a busy garage was fun. There were always plenty of other cars to chat to, and Bertie himself was regularly serviced and maintained and cleaned. Jimmy saw to that.

Several times a year, Bertie would be taken on holiday, quite often to somewhere in Europe, with Jimmy and his friend, Fruity Frobisher. Best of all, Bertie liked the long straight tree-lined avenues of France, where he could get up a really good speed.

The greatest fun Bertie had in those carefree far-off days was to go on car rallies. With Jimmy driving and Fruity Frobisher map reading, Bertie had to find his way at a steady speed over strange roads to distant checkpoints. He always arrived at exactly the correct time and in perfect condition.

Then finally, Bertie would have to do speed tests over mountain roads and round hairpin bends.

'What a magnificent, steady car,' the people would gasp as Bertie went by – usually to win, of course!

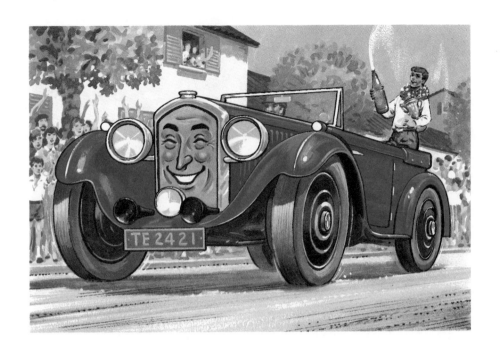

After winning one very important car rally, Bertie drove through the streets of a town in France with Jimmy Taylor sitting up on the back waving a bottle of champagne at the crowds of cheering people.

'This is wonderful!' thought Bertie, 'I'm sure I don't know why anyone is *ever* miserable. Life is a *grand* affair.'

It was really easy for Bertie to be steadfast and strong, while he was being so well treated!

'Thank you! Thank you!' he beamed at the crowds.

To tell the truth, Bertie was becoming rather spoiled. It was only his natural good nature and steady character which saved him from becoming unbearable.

'Oh yes, well, I usually *do* win, actually!' he would remark to other cars – and they could hardly accuse him of boasting, because he was telling the truth.

Wherever they went, Jimmy always saw that Bertie spent the night in a warm garage and was well cleaned.

'Quite right!' Bertie would think. 'I deserve it in return for being so reliable.'

The years went happily by and one summer, Bertie noticed that a young lady named Pam was coming for rather a lot of drives with Jimmy and himself. Pam was very nice and Bertie was pleased when Jimmy announced that he was going to marry her.

On the day of the wedding, Bertie dashed to and fro between the house and the church, taking everyone where they wanted to go.

'How would they ever manage without me?' thought Bertie, looking proudly across at the wedding party.

Then one day their happiness was sadly interrupted.

'War has been declared, Bentley old pal,' said Jimmy in a serious voice. 'There will be no more petrol for the likes of you, no more holidays, no more rallies, just lots of worry for all of us.'

He drained Bentley's engine, took off his tyres and stood him up on bricks in the garage.

'This must all be a dreadful mistake!' gasped Bertie, who did not really understand the meaning of war. 'This can't be happening to a successful car like *me*!'

A few days later, Pam and Jimmy came out wearing strange khaki-coloured clothes. 'We have joined the army,' explained Jimmy. 'We must go away to help in the war. You will have to be patient and wait here until we return.'

Bertie watched as Pam and Jimmy stood in the gateway of their home, waving goodbye.

'How long will they be gone?' he wondered. 'How long shall I have to stay here all by myself? How long do wars last?' There was no one to answer him.

Poor Bertie was feeling really sorry for himself, when suddenly he heard footsteps and a cheery voice. Looking round, he saw Jimmy's old Auntie Winnie.

'Well, Bertie my boy,' she smiled. 'I am going to keep an eye on you and the house while Pam and Jimmy are away. I don't know anything about cars, but I'm all you've got, so make the best of me.'

Bertie began to feel more cheerful and managed a little smile. Perhaps things would not be so bad!

Auntie Winnie closed the garage for the night.

At first things weren't too bad. Auntie Winnie looked in every day, gave Bertie a dust and stayed for a little chat. But gradually she became too busy with her own work to bother.

One of the panes of glass in the garage window broke. Leaves and dirt blew in. A family of birds nested on top of one of Bertie's black horns.

'I want to be useful,' he sighed, 'but how can I be while I am shut up in here? I wish Jimmy and Pam would come home.'

Then one day, the garage doors were opened and the sun came shining in. Blinking in the bright light, Bertie saw Auntie Winnie with an old gentleman.

'This is the car, Doctor Goodheart,' said Auntie Winnie. 'I'm sure Jimmy will not mind if you use it. We all have to do our bit in wartime, even Bertie.'

Bertie's heart leapt. Did this mean he would be taken out of the garage and put back on the road again? He did hope so.

'I will try him,' said Doctor Goodheart.

'Wonderful!' gasped Bertie, feeling happier and happier, as his tyres were put back on. Then he was rolled out into the fresh air and oil and petrol were poured into his engine. Special shades were fitted over all his lamps, so he could hardly be seen after dark.

All the proper mechanics had gone away to the war and only the apprentice, Tommy, was left to service Bertie's engine. He did not know how to do it properly, but Bertie did not complain. He was so happy to be working again. Why worry about a few loose screws?

'Now, Bertie my lad,' said Doctor Goodheart, 'my old car is worn out and I need you to drive me round to visit my patients. A doctor's work is very important and I rely on you not to let me down.'

'I won't,' vowed Bertie, and in spite of the bad servicing he started bravely and drove steadily round the country lanes, never complaining for a moment about the aches and pains caused by the rattling screws.

It was so good to be out again, and to see children playing in the cottage gardens.

Usually Doctor Goodheart looked after sick people in the village, but sometimes, when there was an air-raid on the nearby town, he was called in to help. Then, he would fetch Bertie from his garage and they would drive through the night, lit up only by search lights and by the flames of burning houses.

Even though Bertie ached and grated from bad servicing and poor oil, he would start up and drive steadfastly through the cold night. He had enjoyed the good times. Now he must help in the bad times!

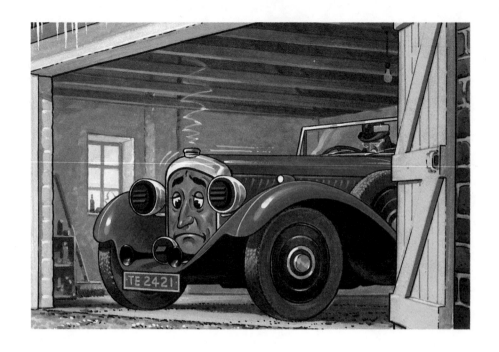

However, the day came at last when even a car as brave and strong as Bertie could no longer fight against all the wrong things that had been done to him.

'WHEEEE! WHIRRRR! CHOKE! GASP!'

No matter how Bertie heaved and struggled, he could not start. Doctor Goodheart sat in the driving seat pulling and pushing at every knob and lever he could see, in an effort to get Bertie going.

'Eeeeek! Ouch! Stop! That hurts!' shrieked Bertie. '*Please* send for a mechanic!'

By that time even young Tommy had gone off to the war.

'Heaven help the army if Tommy is servicing their cars,' thought Bertie.

The only mechanic left in the village was Mister Oilygrin. He was a good mechanic all right, but he was not an honest man. Bertie did not like the look of him when he arrived at the garage.

'Try to get this car started for me, please,' said the Doctor, pointing at Bertie.

Doctor Goodheart went off to make a phone call and Mister Oilygrin lifted Bertie's bonnet. He smiled his horrible oily grin.

'Why, what a magnificent car,' he muttered. 'Nothing wrong with it that proper treatment won't put right. But I will tell the Doctor it is useless.'

Bertie the Bentley could hardly believe his ears. If he was a magnificent car with nothing wrong with him, why should Mister Oilygrin say he was useless?

Mister Oilygrin shut Bertie's bonnet and laughed.

When Doctor Goodheart came back from making his phone call, Mister Oilygrin told him: 'This Bentley is all worn out, doctor. You had better find another car. I will put him back up on his bricks and leave him for Mister Taylor to get rid of at the end of the war.'

'Oh dear! What a nuisance! Well, thank you for your help, Mister Oilygrin,' said Doctor Goodheart, who knew nothing about car engines.

Bertie had never felt so puzzled. Why was Mister Oilygrin telling such lies? He soon found out!

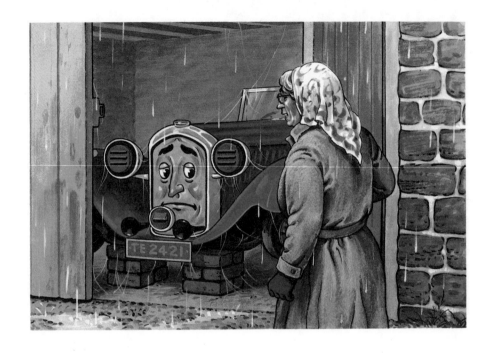

As soon as the doctor was out of the way, Mister Oilygrin re-opened Bertie's bonnet. 'Now,' he chuckled, rubbing his hands and grinning to himself, 'I will take all the best parts from this engine and make lots of money selling them as spare parts. By the time Jimmy Taylor returns home and discovers what has happened, I shall be far away.'

He did as he said and once more Bertie was left in the care of Auntie Winnie, who had no idea of the terrible thing that had happened.

Bertie spent month after lonely month in the cold garage. In the old days it had been easy for him always to be cheerful and happy. But now it needed all his strength of character not to get downhearted. All he could do was to wait, and be brave and hopeful and patient.

Then, one day, Bertie heard the sound of boots crunching on the ground of the yard outside. The garage doors were flung open and in strode Jimmy Taylor. The war was over!

'It's great to see you, Bentley my lad,' grinned Jimmy. 'Goodness knows when we shall ever get any petrol for a run out, but let's have a look at you. I don't believe all this nonsense Auntie Winnie is talking, about you being unreliable and broken down.' He opened Bertie's bonnet and gasped in amazement.

'Someone has taken half your parts away,' he said. 'Why it must have been that rascal, Oilygrin!'

He patted Bertie kindly on the bonnet.

'Don't worry. I'll put you right again,' he said.

Bertie slept more happily that night than he had done for months. He knew that now Jimmy was back, his troubles were over.

A few days later Jimmy's wife Pam also returned home from the war. She laughed when she saw Jimmy out in the yard, surrounded by tools and grease and rags and with his head tucked under Bertie's bonnet.

'It didn't take you two long to get back together again,' she said. But it was many months before Jimmy could find all the parts needed to make Bertie fit.

However, at last the great day came when Bertie was well enough to go on a long run.

'My brother, Sir Smiley Smoothdeal, has written to invite us to spend Christmas with him at Whiteporch Manor,' said Pam. 'He is goodnatured and works very hard to keep the old family house going. Let's drive Bertie down to stay with him.'

So, as daylight was fading, Bertie, Jimmy and Pam found themselves on the long driveway leading to Whiteporch Manor.

Many years later, Jimmy and Pam and Bertie would all come to live at Whiteporch, but they did not dream of that yet. Pam's brother was waiting for them at the porch, which was all decorated with pretty coloured lights ready for Christmas.

'Welcome,' said Sir Smiley, 'my son, Alec, is waiting inside to say "hello" to his Aunt and Uncle.'

He pointed at Bertie. 'Surely you're not still using that old wreck!' he laughed. 'It's time you bought a new car. That one should go to the scrap yard.'

Bertie felt very hurt – and worried too. He was getting old. He might not be as fit as he used to be, especially after all his troubles. Perhaps it was selfish of him to want to go on driving round with Jimmy and Pam. Perhaps they *should* have a younger car!

Jimmy put Bertie away in a warm garage with a cosy oil heater, and wrapped a tartan blanket over his bonnet.

That night it snowed and it snowed. The telephone lines were all weighed down and stopped working.

Sleeping snugly in his warm garage, Bertie knew nothing of the bad weather until, in the small hours of the morning, Jimmy came running in, dragging on his overcoat. 'Wake up, Bentley!' he called. 'We're in trouble and I reckon you are the only car that can help. Sir Smiley has fallen ill and must go to hospital. The phones aren't working and there's deep snow everywhere. Someone has to get through it to take him to a doctor.'

Bertie struggled to wake up.

'Now is the time to show I can be as strong and trustworthy as I was in my youth,' thought Bertie.

He roared his engine into life, blazed out with all his lights, swept up his hood to keep out the snow, and drove with Jimmy to the front of Whiteporch.

Poor Sir Smiley, wrapped in a blanket, was carried out to Bertie's back seat.

'Don't worry,' smiled Jimmy. 'Bertie and I will get you through. There isn't a more reliable car than my old Bentley. The snow won't worry him.'

Even for a great-hearted car like Bertie, the weather was fearsome. The snow lay so thickly on the ground, it was difficult to see where the road ended and the fields began.

Bertie dreaded that at any moment he might lurch into a ditch and be unable to get out again. The icy wind tried to freeze Bertie's engine into silence. The snow slithered under his wheels.

'I will *not* let Jimmy down! I *will* get through,' vowed Bertie, gripping the road and rolling on.

At last they reached the hospital and Sir Smiley was carefully helped inside.

Jimmy Taylor turned to pat his faithful Bertie on the bonnet. 'You got us here!' he said. 'I *knew* you would. There will never be another car like you. We will stay together always.'

Bertie felt so proud! Thanks to his efforts the doctors were able to save Sir Smiley's life and reunite him with his family in time for them all to have a very happy Christmas.

MAURICE MINOR

Maurice Minor
is a reliable little blue car who lived
a quite life in the countryside with
elderly Mrs Conway. This is the
story of how Maurice moved to
town and began an exciting new
life filled with adventures.

Maurice Minor, the little blue car, set out one lovely Spring morning with his owner, Mrs Conway. 'Shopping as usual, I suppose,' he thought.

They left their whitewashed cottage and drove between old stone walls towards the main road.

'Munch! Munch! Munch!' called Maurice to the sheep, grazing with their lambs in the field. 'Don't you get bored with eating grass all day?'

'No. BAAA!' replied the sheep. 'Don't you get bored with chugging round the same old roads?'

Maurice never did get bored with chugging round the roads of the Lake District, where he and Mrs Conway lived. However on that day, to his surprise, instead of driving to the shops, Mrs Conway went on a long trip to visit her son and grandchildren.

'How pretty the flowering cherry trees are at this time of the year,' thought Maurice, as they drew up outside the house where the younger Conways lived.

'Hallo, Grandma. Hallo, Maurice,' called Harry, running out to meet them.

Mrs Conway's visit lasted several days. Then, to Maurice's amazement, she said to him: 'Maurice, I have decided to give you to Harry. I am sure it is a surprise and you must not be upset. Harry has just passed his driving test and needs a well-balanced little car to help him gain more experience. A big powerful car could be dangerous for him. You will be able to help him a great deal.'

Harry was just as surprised, and thrilled too. 'Oh thank you, Grandma. My very own car!' he beamed.

Maurice was not sure whether to be pleased or upset. He liked Harry, but would he like his new home?

Harry and Maurice drove Mrs Conway to the railway station and put her on a train back to the Lake District.

'Goodbye, Grandma and thanks again for Maurice,' shouted Harry to Mrs Conway, who waved from her carriage.

Maurice stood neatly between the white lines in the station car park. He felt quite excited.

'I did like living away in the quiet countryside,' thought Maurice, 'but I suppose it was rather dull. Down here in this big town, things should be much more exciting and lively.'

Harry reversed Maurice, then drove carefully towards the car park exit where two of his friends saw him. 'Harry!' they shouted, hammering on Maurice's roof. 'What are you doing in that car?'

'It's mine!' Harry boasted very proudly, stopping and getting out. 'Isn't it great!'

'Oh, NO!' groaned Maurice. He knew that Harry should not have stopped in the exit from the busy station car park, but no matter how much he revved and coughed, the boys took no notice.

'How marvellous! You *are* lucky! Will you take us for a ride?' burbled the friends.

'TOOT! TOOT! Out of the way please!' hooted an angry red car, pressing up behind them.

'You don't *own* the car park, you know," screeched an impatient saloon behind that, hooting noisily.

Harry hastened out of the station car park and drove Maurice carefully home. 'I can drive,' he said, 'but I still have a lot to learn. You will have to be patient with me, Maurice.'

'Very well,' chugged Maurice, in agreement.

There was no room for Maurice in the family garage and he spent a lot of time standing in the driveway. He became friendly with the big, brown dog, Saxon, who lived next door.

'Good morning,' Saxon would bark over the fence.

One day Maurice overheard Harry chatting to Saxon and George Carter, who lived next door with his father.

'I am not going to live here any more,' George was saying. 'I hate town life and have bought a little farm in the country. I am going to move there and take Saxon with me. He is too big for Dad to manage on his own. The country will be just the place for him.'

Maurice felt very doubtful. He knew how much Saxon loved old Mr Carter, George's father.

Needless to say, George did not ask Maurice's opinion about the move, and a few days later he put Saxon into the back of his car and drove off to his farm in the country.

Old Mr Carter waved goodbye from in front of his house, while Saxon stared forlornly from the rear window of George's red car.

'No good will come of this,' thought Maurice, 'no matter how nice that farm is, nor how kind young George tries to be.'

The days went by. Maurice led a very happy life with Harry, but he heard that Saxon could not settle in the country and was moping. Finally, George sent word that Saxon had disappeared altogether. No one could find him.

Then, one morning at dawn, Maurice opened sleepy eyes to see a thin, scruffy, exhausted dog limping past the front gate. It was Saxon!

As Maurice watched, the bedraggled dog fell to the ground, too hungry and thirsty to go a step further!

'Poor Saxon has found his way home,' thought Maurice. Then he began to feel anxious. Saxon lay on the cold, hard pavement without moving.

Taking a deep breath, Maurice forced a TOOT TOOT from his horn.

Lights went on in the houses, then Harry came running out to see what was wrong. Old Mr Carter looked from his window.

'It's Saxon!' Harry called out. 'He's in a terrible state. You had better come down, Mr Carter.'

Somehow, brave Saxon had found his way for miles and miles to reach his former home and master.

Old Mr Carter nursed the faithful dog back to health and promised that he would never be sent away again. Maurice felt very pleased.

However, Mr Carter was not as young as he used to be and on the days when he did not feel like walking, Harry and Maurice took Saxon for long romps on the hills.

'You're a real friend, Maurice,' woofed Saxon.

Spring gave way to Summer, and Maurice became
quite a busy little town car. He loved the excitement of
running round with Harry and his young friends.

Then a very important day arrived. It was Harry's
first day at work. His father bought him a proper suit.
His mother gave him a white office shirt and a new tie.
Mrs Conway sent a smart briefcase. Maurice waited
outside, polished and spotless.

'Looking smart for business is very important,' said
Harry's parents, as they saw him off.

It was Maurice's job to drive Harry to and from work every day. On that first morning, they arrived early to make a good impression. They went into the car park behind the office block where Harry was to work.

'I wonder if this is right?' thought Maurice. 'All these parking slots are numbered, and I don't know which number is for me.'

Then they noticed the gatekeeper running out of his hut, calling to them. 'Come back!' he shouted.

Harry parked Maurice neatly and got out, watched by the other cars. 'I know this is a private car park for people who work in the offices,' he said politely to the gatekeeper, 'but don't worry. I have just started to work here. This is my first day.'

'That may be,' replied the gatekeeper, 'but you still cannot park here. These parking slots are for *important* members of the staff, not newcomers like you. You must park your car out in the street, until you have worked your way up in the company.'

Feeling very small, Harry and Maurice slunk out of the car park and found a place at the side of the road. At lunch time Harry went to see if Maurice was well.

'Sorry, old chap,' he said, patting the car. 'I know it's noisy and dirty here, but what can I do?'

Maurice smiled bravely although his head ached.

At that moment, an elderly gentleman stopped to admire Maurice. 'Fine little car!' he said, 'but you shouldn't leave it parked in this busy road all day. It might get knocked by a passing lorry.'

'Oh, I know,' agreed Harry. 'I hate leaving him here, but I have just started work in those offices and there is no room for Maurice in the car park.'

'Nonsense!' said the elderly gentleman. 'Of course there is room for a well-kept little thoroughbred like this. I once had one like him myself. Come with me, I own all this property.'

So saying he strode off to find the gatekeeper. In no time at all a space was cleared.

'What a stroke of luck!' thought Harry.

So, the first day at work was a big success. Maurice had a snug parking spot and Harry managed to please his employers with his work.

But the very next morning – oh dear! The postman brought a letter saying that Maurice needed a new tax disc. Maurice had to pass his Ministry of Transport test!

'Maurice!' gasped Harry. 'I forgot that you were old and needed testing! What a nuisance! You must go for a test immediately, or I cannot drive you any more.'

Poor Harry had to miss his breakfast and rush off to the office by bus. He did not want to be late on his second day at work.

His mother had to abandon all the jobs she wanted to do and drive Maurice to the garage to be tested. She handed the car keys to a mechanic.

'He is a sound little car,' she said. 'I am sure there is nothing wrong.'

'That's what they all say,' sighed the mechanic, as he took Maurice into the testing shed.

Of course, Maurice had been for tests before, but that had been with his old friend, Mr Handyspanner at the local 'Keep 'em Rolling' garage in the Lake District. This big town garage seemed rather tough and heartless.

Maurice gritted his teeth. 'I *will* pass, for Harry's sake,' he thought.

He stopped and started his engine, and shone his headlamps and flicked his indicator light exactly when asked. In no time at all Maurice passed his test.

So, Maurice got his new tax disc and soon it was time for the summer holidays. Harry decided to go away with his friend from the office, Bobby.

'Let's go camping for a few days,' suggested Harry, 'and then on to stay with my grandma.'

Maurice was very pleased. 'It will be lovely to see my old owner, Mrs Conway, again,' he thought.

They set off towards the Lake District, past the familiar green fields surrounded by low stone walls.

'Just like old times,' chugged Maurice Minor.

Neither Harry nor his friend, Bobby, knew very much about camping. They left it till almost nightfall before they tried to find a place to pitch their tent.

Luckily, as the shadows were lengthening, they came to a farm. Harry pulled up in the farmyard and went to speak to the farmer. 'You may camp in the second meadow on the right, down the lane,' he said, 'and be careful to close the gate behind you.'

Bobby yawned sleepily. Maurice felt tired too, he had driven a long way that day.

Harry climbed back into the driving seat and nosed Maurice down the lane. 'Second meadow on the left,' he sighed. 'What a kind farmer! I'm too tired to drive another inch.'

'On the left. On the left?' queried Maurice to himself. 'I could have sworn the farmer said "on the right". Oh well, I must have been mistaken, I suppose.' But Maurice had not been mistaken.

On they went down the lane, for quite a long way till they found the gate into the second meadow.

By the time Harry and Bobby had unpacked their new red tent, the daylight was completely gone. Luckily a full moon was shining brightly, and they could just see enough to put up the tent. Then, exhausted, they clambered into their sleeping bags and fell asleep. Maurice closed his eyes, thankful that the long day and the long journey were all past.

Suddenly SCREECH! WHOOSH! An express train thundered by. Nothing could sleep through all that noise! The trains roared past all night long.

Poor Maurice hardly slept a wink and neither did the boys. As the sun rose, they were glad to get up. A brown and white cow came to look at them.

'MOOOO!' she said over the wall. 'You are camping in the wrong field. That field is far too noisy.'

'A pity you could not have told us that last night,' groaned Maurice. 'And now would you mind not mooing quite so loudly. I have rather a bad headache.'

Harry and Bobby managed to cook a nice breakfast, then, after thanking the farmer, they went on their way.

The sun was shining and Maurice tried to roll merrily along the road, but he was too sleepy to do his best. The boys were tired too.

'I think we had better call today a rest day after that bad night,' said Harry. He drove down to a sandy beach and left Maurice safely parked while he and Bobby went to doze near the sea.

'This is a *real* holiday,' smiled Maurice, as the seagulls circled overhead, families played in the sun, and yachts and a big ship sailed by.

Maurice and Bobby and Harry all fell into a deep sleep. SCREEEECH! Hours later the calling of a seagull woke Maurice with a start. He looked towards the beach and gasped with alarm.

The families had all gone. Only Harry and Bobby were still lying on the sand. The tide was coming in fast and the waves of cold water were about to wash over the boys and their belongings.

'TOOOOT! TOOOOT! *TOOOOOOT*!' shrieked Maurice. Just in time the boys woke up.

What a narrow escape! Harry and Bobby were glad to scramble back into Maurice and scuttle on their way. That night they went to a proper camping site, before heading off to visit Harry's grandma.

'Here is Mrs Conway's lane,' revved Maurice, as they reached the turning he had driven up so often with Harry's grandma. He looked fondly at the sheep, the cow and her calf, the girls on horseback, the hikers, the load of yellow hay. It was lovely to be back!

But Harry drove on without stopping!

'Why aren't we visiting Mrs Conway?' gasped Maurice, stalling and trying to turn back.

'I don't know what's come over Maurice,' said Harry. 'He doesn't usually play up like this.'

On they drove to the next town, where Harry pulled up outside a pretty little house. What a surprise! There was Mrs Conway, waving at them. And there was the old cat, Mouser, too.

'How do you like my new home, Maurice?' she called. So that was it! Mrs Conway had moved!

The boys unloaded and went inside. Mrs Conway stayed to show Maurice a present she had bought.

'I hadn't the heart to choose another car after I gave you to Harry,' smiled Mrs Conway. 'So I came to live here in the middle of town, where I didn't need to drive. But I often think about you and I have bought you these nice new seat covers, as a present.'

Maurice was so pleased. He loved his exciting new life with Harry, but it was nice to think Mrs Conway still remembered him. *He* would never forget *her*!